Cover: Angel Walker

EXQUISITE READS PRESENTS

Diaries of the Heart:
Laced with Joy & Pain
The Short Story Collection

Patti Doss

Author's Note

Live. Laugh. Love. Write.

Thanks to all my readers and supporters. This literary industry is definitely not as easy as some people think, but dedicated friends, family, and loyal readers makes it all worthwhile. I truly appreciate your support on this writing journey and I do not take it for likely that you enjoy my works.

Authoress Patti Doss

BRAND ME

Never judge a book by its cover is a popular saying, but does that same principle apply when it comes to relationships?

Meet Draya, a college girl who's always wrapped up in her studies, leaving little time for anything else, especially love. Draya meets Dakari who is definitely sexy and handsome but his perceived bad boy image and occupation turns her off.

Will Draya give Dakari a chance to love her or will she shut him down based on what she thinks love should look like?

TABOO LOVE

You can't help who you fall in love with. Love has no color!

Love doesn't always happen the way we want it. Logan has always had to choose between his choice to love whomever he wants and his father's approval.

After he meets Sariyah, he immediately falls for her, but is worried that his father will not approve. In a world of black and white, there are no gray areas and when it comes to love, there are no exceptions!

Will Logan be with Sariyah or will he let his father's opinion on who he should love deter him?

When Love Runs Out

What do you do when the spark in your marriage is gone?

That's the question that has Danai wavering between her decisions daily. The hurt, pain, and betrayal she endures at the hands of her family and her husband, who is supposed to love and protect her, sends her on a path of depression.

The road of depression continues to unravel until she is faced with the hardest decision of her life. On a mission to get back to herself, revive the happiness she once felt, Danai goes on a journey to find answers.

Will she give her marriage another chance or will she let it all go to start anew?

Brotherly Love

What happens when the love of your life is the brother of an ex and already in a relationship?

Paige met the love of her life in high school, but little did she know he was the half-brother of Kelvin, her once upon a time friend with benefits. After falling for Shaun, Paige ends her fling with Kelvin. However, life happens and Shaun and Paige grew apart and eventually moved on to other people. Despite that, something would always bring them back to each other. Convinced that they are meant for each other, Paige and Shaun work towards being in each other's lives.

With them both already in committed relationships, along with Kelvin's desire to win Paige's heart over his brother, can Paige and Shaun finally be together?

Brand Me

"Come on, Draya. Come go to this tattoo party with us. You don't have to get a tattoo done," Briana said.

"Girl, you know she ain't going to go nowhere. All she wants to do is sit in the house and watch *Lifetime* and *Hallmark* channel all day long," Aniyah interjected.

"Whatever, I just don't want to go, okay?" I said.

"Girl, it's the weekend. We're in college. You're a straight A student, one party won't kill you, I promise! We're supposed to go out and have fun!" Briana stated while walking over and turning off the TV.

"What you do that for?" I questioned.

"Because you going out with us! Now, come on and let's find you something to wear!" Briana replied grabbing my arm, pulling me off the bed.

Although, I rarely went out, when I did, I was always on fleek and my makeup was flawless. If I didn't become a nurse, then I definitely wanted to be a makeup artist for celebrities.

After about an hour, we were leaving to go to the tattoo party. I pulled my crochet Senegalese twists back into a classic bun. I wore my purple skater dress with aquamarine and white striped wedges, aquamarine jewelry, and an aquamarine clutch bag. Of course, I had to have the purple and aquamarine eyeshadow that I paired with purple ombre lips. The aquamarine on my eyes complemented my hazel eyes and caramel skin. The swoop neck of the dress had my 40 C breasts sitting out more than I wanted and my ass wasn't any better. For some reason today, it wanted to look extra big and curvy, causing the already short dress to appear shorter.

Briana had on black leggings with a black cropped top with FLAWLESS written across it in metallic gold letters and black leather high heel sandals trimmed with gold. She loved leggings and I think she had like fifty black pairs. Briana had one of those Kim Kardashian booties except hers was real. For some reason, she loved wearing tights so her phat ass could jiggle. She paired gold accessories and natural looking makeup to correspond with her outfit. Her cocoa skin was already spotless, so she really didn't need over the top makeup. Her breasts weren't big, but her small waist and big ass made up for her lack of breasts.

Aniyah had on some black and white striped casual shorts with a royal blue sheer shirt with royal blue high heels and black accessories. She had long legs like a model and with her petite frame and light skin, people always mistook her for a model.

We arrived at the tattoo party, which looked like just another house party to me. The party was live, though. People were everywhere, the food looked good, and the bar was full. I didn't trust other people's cooking, so I headed to the bar to get me a drink. As I approached the bar, I saw a fine, dark-skinned brother standing near the kitchen island where the bar was set up. He had on a black fitted cap with a black polo shirt, black cargo shorts, and a pair of black and red jays. His left arm was covered in tattoos, and when he turned to the right, I saw a name tattoo on his neck.

I moved closer to the bar and asked the bartender to give me a vodka and cranberry. While waiting for my drink, I felt the guy watching me from head to toe. I looked at him and for a split second, our eyes met. I quickly looked away and prayed for the girl to hurry up with my drink. It wasn't the fact that he was staring, it was more of the fact that he was fine as shit, and I wanted to stare at him. The bartender finally brought my drink and I started to walk away, but he grabbed my arm.

"Excuse me, ma! Why you leaving so quickly? I want to talk to you for a minute. Normally, a guy like that couldn't say two words to me, but his voice was as sexy as his face and deep as his eyes that were so dark they looked black.

"Okay, talk!" I said with a slight attitude.

"No need for the attitude. I just was going to tell you that you look really nice, but that's okay! Enjoy the party," he said and walked off leaving me standing there with the eat ass look on my face.

I couldn't believe he just walked away from me like that. I guess I was so used to being chased that I expected everyone to chase me, but he just switched it up on me really quick and I didn't even get his name.

I drank my vodka and cranberry and went in the direction of the mystery guy. I found him in the living room talking to a tall, light-skinned chick with long,

Brazilian tresses that could pass for a model. They seemed to be engaged in a deep conversation. So, I walked off to find Briana and Aniyah to see if they were still planning to get a tattoo done.

Briana and Ariana was in the den area where the DJ were set up and a small dance floor. I found the pair on the dance floor, Whipping and Nae Nae-ing. After the song was over, I asked them about the tattoos because I hadn't seen anyone set up doing tattoos, yet. I wasn't going to get one, but I wanted to know how long we were going to be at the party. Secretly, I was ready to go. I felt so out of place like I didn't belong and the incident with the guy in the kitchen just proved that this wasn't my type of setting.

We all went back into the living room, where a crowd was gathering around something in the center of the room. We made our way to the front of the crowd and there was the mystery man setting up his table, getting ready to tattoo the girl I saw him talking to!

"Bitch, what's wrong with you? You look like somebody stole your best friend!" Briana joked.

"Nawl, it looks like she got the hots for the Tatt Man!" Aniyah emphasized.

"You're both wrong. Nothing is wrong with me and that guy is not my type," I said, strongly trying to convince them that I was telling the truth. "So, are you guys still getting a tattoo?"

"Yeah," they said in unison.

"We were going to get separate tattoos, but maybe we should all get friendship tattoos. Draya, you have to get a tattoo with us. It wouldn't be right if just Briana and I got one. We're a trio, not a duo, so we have to do it together."

"I don't know, guys. It may hurt!"

"Girl, I have about three tattoos already and it's not that bad. I promise!" Briana declared. "Plus, Dakari is really good. It only hurts for a little while. He did all of my tattoos."

"He did my last one," Aniyah said.

"Okay, so what design do you guys have in mind and where you getting it?" I asked.

Briana showed me a picture of an open safety pin with three red hearts on someone's wrist. "I was thinking this tatt right here and get it on our wrist also with our initials, B.A.D. where the pin is about to close."

"Aww! That's cute! Okay, we can do that, but I'm going last," I said.

"Draya, you are so scary. Girl, I wish you would loosen up for once and live!" Aniyah said.

"Whatever, Aniyah. Since you love to talk, why don't you tell me about Mr. Tattoo Man.?"

"Why?"

"Because I want to know who is going to be sticking me with needles, that's why!" I said hoping she believed that response.

"Oh, I thought you were getting a little crush on Dakari!"

"Girl, you know she don't like thugs! She into those nerdy types that like to sit at home, and build and blow up shit!" Briana said jokingly.

"Whatever!" I said as I watched Dakari finish the rose tattoo on the girl's arm.

He was doing it so effortlessly and carefully. You could see the passion on his face that he loves what he does and it shows. The rose tattoo with pearls on the girl's arm was perfect. You would think she got it done at the shop. Seeing her tattoo, gave me confidence in his skills, but I was still nervous about being so close to him.

"Who's next?" Dakari asked in his sexy ass voice.

"We are!" Briana screamed at him while getting in the chair.

"Girl, you gone be tatted up after a while!" Dakari said to Briana.

"Whatever, man. Just do your job. We want this tattoo on the inside of our right wrists with the initials B.A.D," she said while showing him a picture of the tattoo on her phone.

"What the letters stand for?" he asked.

"Our names, Briana, Aniyah, and Draya."

Dakari nodded and in no time finished Briana and Aniyah's tattoo. Finally, it was my turn. I was so nervous, especially after the little incident in the kitchen.

"Draya, is it? You ready? Just relax and try not to move so much. It's going to sting a little like a shot, but it will quickly go numb. Just try not to move a lot because when you move, you make the needles go deeper than they have to. If the pain gets to be too much, just let me ok, beautiful?" Dakari whispered to me.

Beautiful... So, he was checking for me! Damn.

Dakari did my tattoo and it didn't hurt at all. He was such a professional. Being that close to him had my hormones on fire! Everything I felt whether it was his breath on my face or the smell of his cologne, I was melting inside and when he talked to me. I just wanted to fall into his chest and attack his lips. This man had me feelings things I'd never felt for a man, and considering the fact that he was the complete opposite of the type of guys I normally dated just had me discombobulated for a while. As I paid him for my tattoo, he gave me my change, slipped his card in between my dollars, and winked at me. I just smiled and walked off. We stayed at the party a little while after that, but then we left and went home.

I couldn't wait to get home to text Dakari. Of course, I didn't tell Briana or Aniyah, but there was no harm in seeing where things could possibly go.

I texted him a simple message, *this is my number, Draya.*

He texted back, *OK!*

I figured he must've been still doing tattoos, so I went to bed.

I woke up in the morning to two text messages from Dakari. The first one was timed 1:08 a.m. It read, *Sorry, I'm just now leaving the tattoo party. Everybody wanted a tattoo, but I'll hit you tomorrow and we can go get breakfast or something, so I can get to know the real you and without that protective barrier you got up.*

The second text was from 7:13 a.m., *Good morning, beautiful. Wanna get some breakfast with me?*

I looked at the clock and it was almost eight. I texted Dakari back and told him yes, I would have breakfast with him. I got dressed and met him at IHOP because I didn't want him picking me up from home and risk Briana and Aniyah seeing him.

We ordered our food and talked. Dakari was really easy to talk to and it helped that he was so damn sexy. I

22

tried my best to avoid looking in his eyes because I swear it felt like I was getting lost in them every time I looked into them.

Surprisingly, he didn't fit the stereotypes of most tattoo artists. He didn't act hood. He didn't smoke or drink, which was a huge plus in my book. He was educated, which was another big plus. He talked about poetry, neo-soul artists, social issues within the black community, and much more. The more he talked, the more I was drawn to him. It was as if he was too good to be true.

After we had breakfast that day, we hung a couple more times over the next few weeks. I wouldn't say that we were dating, but we were enjoying each other's company. One day, we were hanging out at his place and I actually let him convince me to get another tattoo. I told him about my dad passing a few months back and how close we were, so Dakari suggested I get a memory tattoo for my father. I decided to get a Cancer ribbon tattoo surrounded by flowers on my chest above my heart. It hurt way more than the tattoo on my wrist, but in a crazy sort of way, the pain felt good. I could see how tattoos could be addictive.

Dakari finished my tattoo, put some A & D cream on it, and softly massaged it into the tattoo. Then, he lifted up his head until we were face to face and he kissed me.

Crazy how we had been kicking for a couple weeks and never once kissed until now. His lips were so soft that I didn't want to stop. Dakari was tearing down all the barriers I had put up with his lips. When we finally broke

the kiss, he immediately started attacking my ears, neck,

and then chest, being careful not to agitate the tattoo area.

The way he was kissing me with a little suction, I was

certain I had marks everywhere. Every kiss was getting

deeper and deeper and although it was a little pain, the

pleasure outweighed the pain. He kissed around the

tattoo and covered my nipple with his mouth while his

hands slid down my pants into my pussy. As his mouth

made love to my breasts, his hand went down into my

warm, wet, sticky center. Just as I was about to release my

love juices onto his fingers, he stopped and got up. He

reached out his hand to me. I put my hand into his and

followed him into the bedroom.

Once we were in the room, he undressed me, piece by piece, stopping to plant kisses in between. After he undressed me, I returned the gesture. After I took off his boxers, his long, thick, dick was slowly coming to life with every touch. By the time he was completely naked, his dick was banging at my pussy's door, only I wasn't ready to let him enter yet. I instructed him to sit on the edge of the bed as I kneeled down in front of him. His chest was covered in tattoos and I tried to kiss each and every one until I was face to face with his beautiful rigid dick. I deposited tiny kisses along the shaft of his dick while slowly massaging his balls. I could tell he was getting anxious, so I kissed the head of his dick before slowly putting it in my mouth inch by inch until my mouth covered the entire thing. He made love to my mouth until his love juices spilled and ran down the back of my throat.

I got up and directed him to lie in the middle of the bed as I straddled him. Once again, his tattoos demanded my attention and I kissed and licked on every one. His lips looked neglected, so I kissed those as well. It was only a peck on the lips because I wasn't sure if he wanted to taste himself, but when I tried to pull away from him, he kissed me harder and deeper while his dick kept hitting against my stomach.

"Condoms?" I asked.

"Top drawer on the nightstand," he replied in between kisses.

I reached over and grabbed a condom, quickly opened and slid it on him. When he entered me, it felt like a perfect fit. I rode him while kissing on his neck and chest until his body started to convulse underneath me. I climbed off him and he sat up, removed the condom and went to flush it. When he returned, I was bent over on the bed with my hands on the headboard and a condom on my back. It didn't him long to get the message and by the time he got behind me, his dick was already standing at attention. He wasted no time in putting on a new condom and thrusting his dick into me. I continued to hold on to the headboard as he thrust in and out of me fast and slow. I tried to match his movements as best I could, but I couldn't. He was in beast mode and he was taking it out on me in the most pleasurable way possible. As he thrust

28

his dick into me, he planted small kisses on my back. He continued beating up my pussy until he had nothing else to give and until his love juice filled the condom. Before he pulled his dick out of me, he kissed me on my back once more. He finally extracted his dick from me and ran his tongue down the middle of my ass while inserting his finger into my still wet and warm center. His hand danced in my pussy until my body convulsed. I laid flat on the bed while he got up to dispose of the condom.

When he returned, he kissed me on the lips. I got up to use the bathroom. When I looked in the mirror, my neck and chest was filled with love marks. It even looked like one was on my jaw. I chuckled to myself, thinking how the hell I was going to explain that big ass mark on my face. As I started reminiscing about how it got there, it made me smile. I used the restroom, washed up as best I could without getting in the shower, and joined Dakari in the bed. He was already halfway asleep and after a while, he was knocked out.

As I outlined his tattoos with my fingers, rubbed my hands over my own tattoos and love marks, I got a wonderful feeling. I didn't know what the future held for us, but I did know that Dakari could *brand me* any day!

"Hurry up, Logan! I'm ready to get this damn grand opening over with so I can get back home! You know how much I hate being over there. If I wasn't the Mayor, I wouldn't be caught dead on that side of town," said James McBride.

Logan rolled his eyes at his father. He hated how his father judged people based on what side of town they lived on. Logan finished dressing and put on his Navy blazer. He had on a baby blue oxford shirt with navy slacks and dark brown loafers. The baby blue shirt matched his eyes and made his eyes appear deeper and brighter. His short cut

"Dad, why do you always do that?" He asked his father as he climbed in to the black SUV with the tinted windows alongside his father.

"Do what, son?" James asked, slightly agitated.

"Talk down on people from the other side of town. Some of those same people you talk about are the very ones that helped put you in office."

James looked at his son with a terrifying stare and said, "I am a third generation Mayor! I was going to be mayor regardless of who voted!

Logan stared out of the window. He knew his father was right. When it came to politics in the town of Masonville, money ruled over democracy. Votes could be bought and elections could be rigged for the favorable candidates to win. That's the way it has always been in Masonville and any righteous candidate never stood a chance to clean up the town because almost everybody in government positions were crooked and there was no room for honesty.

The number of candidates that have tried to run based on a platform of honesty was destroyed by mudslinging, lies, and allegations. Things got so bad, that honest people stopped running for office and moved away.   Not only officials, but majority of the older generations were moving out of Masonville at alarming rates. I guess they felt like going through segregation once in a lifetime was enough and to be constantly stuck in a place that is not growing, while the rest of the world is moving forward was ludicrous.

Secretly, he was praying his father would not start about him being next in line to run the town. He had no interest in becoming mayor. In fact, he wanted to move as far away from Masonville as he could and open up a car garage and work on cars.

Cars were his passion. He loved everything about them and fixing on cars relaxed him in a way nothing else could, but his father hated how much he loved being a mechanic. He felt that being a mechanic was beneath Logan and anyone in the McBride family. He wanted Logan to follow in his footsteps and become a generational mayor of Masonville. Logan did a pretty good job at fooling his dad that he would follow in his footsteps, but in his spare time, he worked as a mechanic for a garage on the other side of Masonville. A side of town his father would never approve of, but Logan loved it. Logan loved interacting with people from different backgrounds and different classes. Being around people other than the rich and snobby, humbled Logan in a way that opened his eyes to issues, he never knew existed, like how hard middle-class people had to work to make ends meet.

They pulled up to the building of the grand opening. It was a hair salon called *X'Quisite Cuts & Curls*. Logan knew that his father would rush through this grand opening because his father dreaded this side of town, as for Logan, he didn't have a problem because most of his clients from the garage lived on this side of town. As they exited the car, the owner came out to greet them. She was a dark-skinned lady about 5'6, 150 lbs., with hazel eyes. She had on a pair of black ankle pants with white glittered heels with a semi-sheer white sweater and a purple chemise underneath. She was gorgeous, but Logan knew he couldn't even think about talking to her outside of business, as long as his father was around.

His father found out about his love for black girls when he came over and caught his ex-Ashley there. Ashley was a 5'7, caramel-skinned cutie with honey colored eyes that he met at his garage. Her car was making loud noises and she wanted to see what it was. It ended up being her driver's side wheel barren. Logan fixed her car and they exchanged numbers. They dated for a while and things were starting to get serious.

One Sunday morning, after Ashley stayed the night. Ashley was cooking Logan breakfast, while he was still sleep. James came over and Ashley opened the door with one of Logan's oxford shirts on and nothing underneath. James was pissed and screamed at Ashley demanding to know who she was and why she was there. Ashley and James argued, which woke Logan up. After coming downstairs and seeing his father and girlfriend going at it, Logan tried to intervene, but instead of standing up for

Ashley, he asked her to leave and told her that he would call her later. Ashley realized that he would never stand up to his father about his love for her or any other woman of color, so she broke up with him and continued her rant to his father about being a racist, corrupt asshole.

The pain of losing Ashley still hurt Logan and because of it, he put dating on the backburner for a while. Seeing the owner of the new shop, had him rethinking that decision. She was simply breathtaking.

"Hello! I'm Sariyah James, the owner of the shop," the beautiful lady said as she reached out her hand to Mayor McBride to shake.

Sensing his father's hesitation, Logan grabbed Sariyah's hand and shook it firmly.

"I'm Logan McBride. Please excuse my father, but he is feeling a little under the weather, so I will be handling the grand opening, if that is okay with you?" Logan stated.

"Miss James, I'm truly sorry. Please forgive me, but my son will take excellent care of you in my absence. I thought I was feeling well enough to attend this event, but I'm afraid I was wrong. I just wanted to tell you in person," Mayor McBride declared and turned to get back into the truck. He looked back at Logan, his eyes telling him not to even think about getting with Sariyah. Logan looked back at him with blank eyes as if he had not heard him or seen the seriousness in his face and turned his attention back to Sariyah.

"Miss James, shall we get this party started?" Logan said holding out his hand to her, while flashing her his beautiful wide smile and small dimples.

Once they entered the shop, everybody stopped what they were doing and started staring at Logan as if he had three heads.

"It's okay, Logan. They're cool, I promise. A lot of them are just never around white people, no offense," Sariyah declared.

"None taken. I understand completely. Before I get to enjoying this wonderful party can we go ahead and do the ribbon-cutting ceremony, so the lady from the newspaper can get the picture?" Logan replied.

Sariyah and her staff gathered with Logan behind the beautiful, large purple ribbon that was tied in a bow in the front of her shop. Being that close to her was making Logan nervous. He didn't want her to think he was purposely trying to get behind her, but the photographer kept telling them squeeze in tight. For a moment, it felt like she wanted him to be all on her because even when she didn't have to, she kept getting closer and closer. By the time they took the picture, Sariyah was so close to him, that he could bend down and kiss the back and side of her neck. Her intoxicating fragrant was driving him nuts, compiled with the way her dress was fitting her, he was trying everything in his power to calm himself before he got a little too excited.

After the ceremony, he handed Sariyah her certificate and congratulated her on her new shop. "Miss James, you have a beautiful shop and I'm sure you going to do just fine. Enjoy the rest of your evening."

"Thank-You! Do you need a ride?" She asked him.

"No, I called for a car to pick me up."

"Well, I wish you would have stayed and mingled a while. I won't bite, I promise. Unless you want me to and I'll be more than happy to oblige!"

Logan's cheeks started to turn red as he couldn't help but blush at the fact that this beautiful chocolate sister was checking him out.

"I'm sorry, I didn't mean to embarrass you. I was just having fun with you. Loosen up, it's a party. So, how about you call your driver back and tell him to hold off on picking you up and I'll personally make sure you have a great time. So, in a sense, I'll be your bodyguard," Sariyah confirmed and laughed.

"Okay, so you're going to protect me?"

"Yes!" She replied with a smirk.

"Protect me from what? I don't see any danger," Logan stated, playing along with her.

"From all these women that are undressing you with their eyes!"

The both burst out laughing and everyone turned to look at them trying to determine what was so funny. Logan's cheeks were warming up again.

"Come on. Have a look inside my office. I didn't want to do an office at first, but then I decided I need a place for myself when I was tired, overworked, or just need to be alone," she informed him while grabbing his arm and leading him to her office.

Logan quickly texted him driver and told him to hold off on picking him up until he called again.

The office was painted a pink beige and had parquet flooring. Light Pink linen curtains hung over the one window in the office. The original lighting of the room had been replaced with a leaf-styled ceiling fan. There was candles everywhere and she had two floor lamps, one in each corner of the room. Near the window, she had a small wooden coffee table with wicker basket drawer fronts and two basket weave chairs with white cushion and pink, beige, and brown pillows. She had a medium-size pine desk on the other side of the room that was shaped like a table you may see in a kindergarten classroom where the teacher sits behind and about four students sit in front of her. The room was so relaxing and the dimmed lights almost made the mood of the room, romantic.

"So, what do you think?" Sariyah asked interrupting Logan's thoughts.

"I like it. The atmosphere is so inviting, so relaxing, so happy!" He replied as he sat in one of the wicker chairs near the window.

"Thanks! That's exactly what I was going for when I designed it," she boasted as she joined him by the window.

"Well, you did an awesome job! The place looks really nice. We probably should get back to your grand opening. We don't want people to think you being rude."

"They will be okay. This is my shop, remember? So, I set my own rules. Do you mind if I take my shoes off for a minute? These heels are killing my feet!"

"As long as your feet don't stink, be my guest," he asserted with a chuckle.

She reached over and playfully hit him.

"I guess I do need to hire you to be my bodyguard, you don't play!" He declared sarcastically.

She took off her shoes, and began rubbing her feet.

He couldn't help but notice her perfectly, pedicured toes, with a purple nail color that matched her chemise. All he could think was she has kissable feet.

"Do you mind if I do that for you?" He asked.

"Do what? Rub my feet?" she inquired skeptically.

"Yes! Rub your feet. I can see that you need a massage and I would be less of a man to sit her and let you do it yourself."

Without waiting on her response, he got on the floor besides the wicker chair she sat in and began massaging her feet. The coffee table was in the way, so he pushed it to the side. Now he was directly in front of her massaging her feet.

Sariyah was melting on the inside at Logan's every touch. No man had ever given her a foot massage. EVER. The fact that a man she barely knew, a white man at that, was willing to rub her aching foot, was turning her on in the worse way. Call her crazy, but she was ready to give herself to him right then. She wasn't the one-night stand or sex on the first date type of girl, but her alter ego was knocking at the door, trying to get out. She squirmed in her seat, readjusting her legs and skirt, so her intimates wouldn't be visible to him as he massaged her feet.

Logan started massage from her feet to her calves and to her thighs. The further up he went, the more she squirmed in her seat.

"Stop me anytime," he raved to her in his sexiest voice.

Looking down at him, she was mesmerized by his rich blue eyes. Her mind and heart was fighting. Her mind was telling her to get up and get out of there, but her body was telling her that she needed and wanted this. Her mind was losing the battle rather quickly as he moved further and further up her dress. She thought he was about to play in her honeypot, but he moved his hand to her stomach, under her shirt, and up to her curvaceous breasts that was almost spilling over her bra. No longer fighting her urge for some white chocolate, she pulled Logan face to hers and kissed him. Midway into the kiss she tried to pull away, but Logan pulled her deeper and deeper into him. She finally stopped resisting and went with the flow. After their tongues played tug-of-war for what seemed like minutes, he started kissing on her cheeks and necks, stopping to suck on her earlobes and the dimples in her collarbone. He whispered in her ear how beautiful she was to him and planted small kisses from her ear back to her lips, before he stopped and got up.

"You do feel as good as you look, but it would be so rude of us to continue to stay held up in your office. It is your grand opening and you should be mingling with your customers and workers. I'll have my driver pick me up, and I'll call you in the morning," he volunteered as he handed her his card.

"How you going to call me and you don't have my number?" She contested.

"I don't have it yet, but you are about to give it to me," he gloated.

Sariyah just giggled and handed him her card. It took her a minute to regain her composure, but she knew he was right. It was not a good look for her to be in her office with him especially with so many people around.

"You'll right. You can wait for your driver in here, if you want and I'll talk to you later," Sariyah stated while walking towards the door.

"Wait a minute," Logan replied and he walked over to her and gave her another big kiss. "Enjoy your party, Miss James."

Before she did something she would regret, she hurriedly left the room and rejoined the party. Logan sat back down and called his driver. He didn't know what it was about Sariyah, but if there was a such thing as love at first sight, he was coming down with a bad case of it.

He called his driver and waited inside her office. After a few minutes, he heard yelling and screaming. He tried to ignore the noise, because it was none of his business, but the screams got louder and louder. Logan finally emerged from the office and found a guy pulling on Sariyah and all in her face yelling at her.

"Leave me along, Craig. I told you that it's over! Get out of my shop!" She was screaming, but the guy wasn't bulging.

"I thought you weren't in there with nobody, Ri-Ri! There that motherfucker goes right there!" Craig specified pointing at Logan.

"He ain't my boyfriend, he is the mayor's son. He came here for the grand opening ceremony!" She screamed at Craig.

Craig let go of her shirt he was pulling on and started walking towards Logan. Logan didn't move, but got into a defensive stance. Sariyah was yelling for Craig to leave Logan alone, but Craig wouldn't listen. He approached Logan and started swearing and yelling in his face. What Craig didn't know was that Logan had a black belt in jiu-jitsu. Craig continued screaming in Logan's face.

"I don't know who you are, but you really need to calm down and leave. Miss James, have already asked you to leave her place of business. If you don't leave, I will have to call the police," Logan voiced through clinched teeth.

He was trying so hard to be a gentleman, but he also didn't want to appear weak in Sariyah's eyes or have Craig think he was afraid of him.

"Call the motherfucking police! You go need 'em and the ambulance, after I whop your ass!" Craig threatened and raised his arm as if he was about to strike Logan.

Logan grabbed Craig's left arm with his right arm and swiftly swung him around. He inserted his left arm under Craig's left arm and reached around to the back of his head, while his right hand held Craig's left arm to his chest and apply light pressure to Craig's neck and in less than ten seconds, Craig fell to the floor.

"Sariyah—Miss James, call the police," Logan stressed as he prepared to walk out the door. He texted his driver that he was ready to go.

"Wait, Logan" Sariyah said and followed him outside. "Thank you for what you did in there for me. Craig is an ex-boyfriend that has been stalking me for…"

"No offense, Miss James, but you don't owe me an explanation for his behavior. He should have never disrespected you or your place of business like that. You should get a restraining order again him, because it's no telling what he is capable of."

"Okay, I will and thank you again for everything. I'm sorry the night ended so badly," Sariyah cited looking down.

Logan walked over to her and placed his finger under her chins and lifted up her head. "My night didn't end badly. I'm standing next to a beautiful, sexy, chocolate goddess. I'd say that's one heck of an ending."

His blue eyes capturing Sariyah's attention again and no longer able to hide the way he was making her feel, she reached up and kissed him. Logan kissed her back, but pulled away as the police pulled in.

"I'll give you a call in the morning, to check on you, Logan declared before walking over to the officer to explain to the officer what happened. The officer then talked to Sariyah, just as Logan's driver pulled up.

"Officer, I'll be down in the morning to give my full statement. Good night, Miss James!" and he disappeared into the back seat of the black Lincoln Town car with the pitch black tint.

***

The next morning, Logan awoke to his father beating on his door. He finally opened the door and immediately wish he hadn't. His father was going on and on about the altercation at Sariyah's shop then he starting talking about Logan's love for black women. Logan drowned out most of the conversation until his father called Sariyah *a black ghetto bitch.*

Logan was livid and for the first time in his life, he finally stood up to his father.

"Dad, you are wrong. Sariyah hasn't done anything to you. You don't even know her. You always want to tear down minorities as if they are less equal than you when the fact of the matter is our graves are going to be the same size. I don't even see how you go through life with so much hatred, it's tiring and lonely. I let you run Ashley away. I should have fought harder to protect her honor, but I didn't because I want to please my father and make him proud of me. The truth, I know you will never be proud of me and I'm okay with that because I don't want your life. I don't want to be a mayor of this corrupt town. Most of my life, I have been ashamed to be your son because of your racist attitude. Well, here's a reality check dad! Most of my closest friends are black. Some are Hispanics and other minorities. A few may even be gay or disable, but they are my friends and you or anyone else can't tell me to stop being their friends. I love black women. I think they are some of the most beautiful women in the world. I have dated white girls, but I prefer dating black girls and if things go well with Sariyah, she's going to be my woman and possibly my wife! So, I'm telling you now if you cannot accept any of that, then you can just leave my house right now!" Logan stated sternly.

His father walked out of the house and slammed the door. Logan locked his door and went back to bed. He couldn't believe he had stood up to his father but he was finally felt at peace. After years of cowering to his father's commands, he finally established his own.

***

Sariyah laid awake all night with Logan McBride on her mind. She has never dated a white man before, but she was seriously smitten with Logan. The way everything played out yesterday left her feeling like she was in a modern-day lifetime movie. She kept beating herself up for not getting his number. Now she was stuck waiting and wondering if he was going to call her.

Just as her mind was starting to accept the fact that she would probably get another chance with Logan, her phone rang. She hurriedly answering her phone without looking at the number, she answered and prayed in her head that it was him.

"Good morning, beautiful! I hope you haven't eaten yet on this lovely, Saturday morning, because I want to treat you to breakfast, since our night together was so rudely interrupted," Logan declared.

Sariyah was so happy that he called her that she hoped up and immediately jumped up and down on the bed.

"Hello! Hello!" Logan cited into the phone.

"Oh, I'm sorry. I'm still waking up, but I would love to go to breakfast with you. I'm starving anyway, especially since I didn't eat much last night."

"Don't remind me about last night. I hated the night had to end. So, how bout you meet me at the mall. You can leave your car there and ride me to get breakfast."

"No! How about you tell me where you want to have breakfast and I'll meet you," she insisted.

Not wanting to make her upset or cause her to cancel on him, Logan agreed.

"Meet me at the Crackel Barrel down from the mall in about thirty minutes. See ya soon, beautiful."

"Okay," she stated and hung up to get dressed for her breakfast date with Logan.

***

When Sariyah got to *Crackel Barrel*, Logan was waiting for her at the entrance. He was dressed down in some black joggers and a white v-neck shirt with some black Nikes, but he still looked handsome as ever. They were twinning without even planning it, she had on black yoga pants, flip-flops, and a white *MUW* t-shirt.

"So, you trying to dress like me, huh?" he uttered to her.

"No, black and white is universal comfort clothes color, I guess!" she replied.

He simply laughed and held the door open for her to enter. After they were inside, he grabbed her hand and held it as they walked up to the hostess to seated.

The hostess was a young, blond that looked as if she was still in high school or just starting college.

"How many?" She asked Logan while looking directly at him, refusing to acknowledge Sariyah that was standing beside him and holding his hand.

Before Logan could answer, Sariyah asserted sternly, "Two!" That caught her attention and she quickly looked from Logan to Sariyah. Logan looked at Sariyah, his eyes telling her to *calm down and let him handle it* but her eyes were giving the waitress the message *to not fuck with her*, but either the waitress was bad at reading eyes and body languages or she really didn't give a damn. After they were seated, she again looked at Logan and told him, "Your waitress will be here shortly," and walked off.

"It's okay, beautiful. I've dealt with plenty of ignorant people like that. Don't let her get too you. Plus, she's just mad that you snagged a sexy, piece of Vanilla!" Logan said while reaching across the table and grabbing Sariyah's hands.

She couldn't help but laugh. "Really? Is that what it is?"

"Yeah, look, she's still staring!" Logan muttered.

"Well, let's not be rude. Let's give her something to look at. Sariyah got out of her chair and leaned over the table and kissed Logan. He kissed her back and they kissed from what seemed like a minute or two. When they finally broke apart and looked up at the hostess stand, the hostess had disappeared. Logan and Serenity burst out laughing.

"Well my appetite just changed for something else. You wanna get out of here, before she has her friends spit in our food or something?" Logan insisted.

"Sure, cause I would hate to catch a case and end up in a cell next to Craig for whopping her ass all over this restaurant."

Just as they were leaving, their waitress was approaching the table.

"We're leaving!" Logan stated and grabbed Sariyah's hands and walked out, with the waitress still standing there looking dumbfounded.

Standing against his car, she asked, "So where are we going to eat?"

Logan stood in front of her and asked, "Do you trust me, Sariyah?"

"Yeah, I guess I do. I feel comfortable around you, maybe too comfortable, because I still barely know you. So, how about we get something quick to eat and you can keep me company, while I clean up my shop. After you left last night, everyone left and I didn't get a chance to clean up. So, it will be like a do-over from last night without all the drama," she replied.

"Sure, I'd love that. I'll pick up us some breakfast from Jack's and I'll meet you back at your shop. You're not allergic to anything that I should about, are you?" Logan inquired.

Sariyah laughed.

"Did I say something wrong?" He asked.

"No, you didn't. Most guys would ask about your allergies when they are offering to get you food, that's all."

"Well, I'm not most guys and if you give me the chance, you are going to see that, I'm one of a kind, a rare breed!" he said and chuckled.

"Alright now, see you at the shop!" She said as she prepared to get in her car.

"Wait a minute," he commanded. He pulled her to him and kissed her with everything in him. She resisted a little because he was holding her so tight, but after a few seconds, she stopped resisting and gave into her own desires for him. They kissed for minutes, before coming up for air.

"Be safe, beautiful."

Sariyah got in her car and pulled off. Watching her pull off, Logan knew two things. One, he was falling for Sariyah James and two, she was going to be MRS. LOGAN MCBRIDE!

WHEN LOVE RUNS OUT

"Danai, you want something to drink?" Jonathan calls from the kitchen.

"No! I'm okay," I answered and continued to watch T.V.

Jonathan comes out of the kitchen with him a mixed drink and bops down on the sofa. I was seated on the loveseat. Even though we were together, we were still very much apart. We were sitting on the couch watching the New Year come in.

No big celebration, no party, not even a glass of champagne. The kids are sleep and not a word is being passed between Jonathan and I. 10, 9, 8, 7, 6, 5, 4, 3, 2, and 1, HAPPY NEW YEAR! It's 2016, but already this year feels like a repeat of 2015. I hear firecrackers and guns blaring in the background. I heard the laughter of people celebrating the New Year outside my window and all I can think is why are they so freaking happy? Why can't I be happy like that?

I remember hearing the New Year's Day song and seeing the many couples onscreen hugging and kissing and smiling and all I could think is what are they so happy about. Bitter right? I know I looked up and I realized I was a bitter ass woman for thinking that way. They are enjoying life and I'm stuck in a loveless marriage.

As always, I feel lost, alone, half of a shell of the woman I used to be. I feel my strength wavering as I think of going through another year in this dead marriage. My heart aches as I hear the continued laughter of life outside my apartment. People laughing and shooting fireworks and having a great time while I'm in the house watching TV and Facebooking.

With each laugh, each firecracker blast, or gunshot into the air, I feel myself sinking deeper and deeper into depression. Knowing the signs, I know that I'm depressed probably have been for a long time, I just kept myself busy so I wouldn't think about it. Plus, when you are a strong person, no one ever asks, "Are you ok?" "How are you doing?" they assume because you were strong for them that you don't need anyone. That's so not true. I used to talk to my sister and get things out instead of keeping everything balled up inside, but lately, she has been so busy with school and work that I haven't seen her in months. We talk maybe once a week on the phone, but it's not like it used to be. Sometimes, I talk to my best friend Sasha about my marriage, but she is in a fresh relationship and I didn't want to bombard her with my issues. So, like I am so used to doing, I internalize my pain and pretend it's not there.

*****

March 2016, feelings from New Year's Day haven't gotten much better. In fact, my situation actually got worse. It takes everything in me to start each day knowing that a piece of me is dying every time. When I say the misery seemed as if it was taking over me I mean it. Jonathan is cheating again. I could tell from the increase in the verbal abuse and his need to keep me from going anywhere or doing anything. I used to drink to block out my problems, but lately, I didn't even have the will to drink anymore. I didn't have the will to do anything. I couldn't even force myself to go to church. I was in a horrible place and people I thought I could turn to or wanted to turn to was nowhere in sight. Another pain hit. Realization of spending my time helping people that wouldn't stop for a minute to help me. After I realized . that this was something I was going to have to do on my own. I prepared myself for the task of leaving my husband mentally and physically. I worked longer hours to save more money to get my own place and my own car. I started documenting everything: dates of arguments, verbal abuse sessions, weekends he wouldn't come home, Facebook messages to other women and inappropriate messages or posts on Facebook about me or our marriage. I was slowly building my case for divorce.

It wasn't until I started noticing things missing from around the house did I realize that Jonathan may have actually been bringing his women to the house while I worked at night. After finally confiding in Sasha, she suggested we set up a hidden camera to gather more information that could possibly help my case in court.

*****

"Are you ready, Danai?" Sasha asked me.

"Nobody could ever be ready for something like this, but I have to know so I might as be ready," I replied.

Sasha started connecting the Nanny Cam to her laptop. For a week, we hid a camera in my living room inside of a clock, now we were about to see what exactly goes on while I'm at work. As she set everything up, the knots in my stomach grew bigger and bigger.

It was her idea to set up a Nanny Cam to catch Jonathan from the beginning. I suspected that Jonathan was having a woman over after I went to work, so she suggested that I set up one. Sasha has been my best friend since college. We met when we were both pledging AKA. Our friendship grew beyond sorority sisters. Sasha became like a real sister to me, more than my biological sister, Diamonique. Diamonique is younger than me, so we don't click on a lot of things. I am a Shift Manager for

Wal-Mart, but I work the night shift while going to school online for my MBA in small business and entrepreneurship. Jonathan works during the day as an automotive mechanic instructor at the Vocational Center.

Sasha finally finished connecting everything and called me over.

"Come on sit down, cause you making me dizzy!" Sasha exclaimed.

I was so nervous; I hadn't even noticed that I had been pacing the floor. I wasn't sure if I was ready to see what was on the video, but I had to know because the not knowing part was driving me crazy. I finally joined Sasha at the kitchen island and took a seat on the bar stool next to her.

The video started playing and I saw Jonathan and the kids arriving home from work/school.

"Can we fast forward this?" I asked Sasha.

Sasha fast forwarded the video until the kids were gone to bed and Jonathan was the only one in the living room.

"Stop right there!" I told Sasha.

Jonathan was on the couch texting someone. The way he was smiling he couldn't have been texting his boys, at least, I hoped not. I looked at the time stamp and quickly checked my phone to see if he messaged me around that time. He had, in fact, texted me, but it was nothing that would cause him to smile like the joker. The message he sent me was simply to tell me about the kids' day and to let me know that he just put them in the bed. He always texts me about their day so that wasn't out of the ordinary. Regardless of what went on between him and me, he was a good father to the kids. He was just a bad husband to me.

We continued to watch the video. At some point, he took a shower because he left off camera for a while and came back, laying on the couch in some gray basketball shorts and no shirt. The camera did him justice because he looked so sexy on the video. His dark chocolate skin, tight abs, and muscles were screaming to be kissed. He grabs his phone again and starts back texting. Once again,

I check the time stamp and check my phone to see if he texted me at that time. No text from Jonathan. He was talking to someone, but who? Sasha fast forwarded through about ten minutes of him texting before resuming the video. Just as the video starts, the doorbell rings and Jonathan gets up to answer it. I look at the time stamp; it is almost eleven. The knots in my stomach wrung up tighter and tighter at the realization that not only was Jonathan cheating on me but the fact that he was doing it in our house.

Sasha immediately paused the video and looked at me. "Are you sure you want to know, Danai?" she asked me.

"Sasha, it's no point of stopping now. Just play it!" I stated as my palms grew hot and sweaty.

Sasha didn't say anything; she just restarted the video. Jonathan gets up and open the door and in walks Diamonique, my pregnant, 21-year-old sister! Sasha and I both looked at each other in shock and back to the video.

My mouth fell open in shock. My heart felt like it was shrinking in my chest while I got a sudden onset of nausea. I tried so hard not to let my emotions show, but I know Sasha saw the hurt and disappointment in my face. Of all the women in the world, it was my sister!

Diamonique had on a thin maxi dress with a cardigan. She came in and as soon as Jonathan locked the door, they embraced and started kissing! Hurt and disappointment turned to anger. With flaring nostrils and grinding my teeth, there was no way to hide my anger. I was beyond pissed. I hopped up off the stool and grabbed my keys and headed to the door. I was going to confront him and my sister, but Sasha blocked the entrance.

"Calm down, Danai! Don't go doing something crazy. Think about your kids. He is not worth you losing your kids over," she said sympathetically but I could hear in her voice that she was just as pissed as I was. I fell to the floor as the realization that not only was my marriage over, but the fact that my sister betrayed me. Sasha sat down on the floor and held me. All the pain I've held in for the last couple of years were coming out and I had no way to stop them. All of the times, I should have left but I kept coming back because I was afraid of being alone was now biting me in the ass.

It felt like I cried on Sasha's shoulder for hours. We finally got up off the floor and after I calmed all the way down, I prepared to leave.

"Can you please make me a copy of that video? Put it on a DVD, please," I said to Sasha.

"Okay, Danai, but what are you going to do with it?" She asked.

"I don't know yet, but I know I'm not going to do anything rash.

"Are you sure you're going to be okay?" Sasha asked as she downloaded the video onto a DVD for me.

"Yes, I'm okay. The video just confirmed suspicions, I've had all along."

"Okay, well call me if you need me."

"Sasha, can you please pick my kids up from school today. I need some time to deal with everything and I don't want them to see me like this. I promise I am not going to mess with Jonathan and Diamonique.

From the video, it's clear that they don't give a fuck about me or my feelings. It doesn't take a rocket scientist to figure out what was going to happen next or to figure out that they have been doing this for quite some time. Now, I understand why my sister hasn't been around lately and why she is always canceling on me when I asked her to go places with me. I just blew it off as her and her friends already had plans or that she just didn't want to hang with her big sister. Now, I know it was because she was fucking my husband! I'm going to go home and start packing me and the kids' things. I refused to stay one more night in that house with him. If I stay, I'm afraid of what I'm going to do to him or to my sister. I need a copy of the video, so I can leave for him to watch and understand why I left.

"Okay, if that's what you want. Just be safe, hun. I love you and remember your kids, no matter what happens.

"I will! Thanks for everything," I said while giving her a hug as I prepared to leave.

I wasn't going to work. I had to deal with the situation at hand. I called my mom and asked her to pick up the kids later from Sasha's house because Jonathan and I both had to work late. She agreed to watch the kids, so I texted Jonathan and told him that the kids were going to spend the weekend at my mom's.

I was hurt. In fact, I was beyond hurt. I was more upset at the fact that he was sleeping with my sister than the fact that he was actually cheating on me. I held my emotions together as best I could, but I couldn't help wondering was it my fault? Did I do something wrong? Was I not attentive enough? Was I not good enough? I wasn't perfect, I knew that, but I tried my hardest to be an excellent wife. I stuck by him, regardless of the cheating rumors and the disrespect. I know I have a smart mouth and I'm sarcastic as hell, but throughout this marriage, I've been nothing but faithful and honest to him. I may be a big girl (5'3 about 185 lbs.), but my curves are in all the right places. I'm smart, beautiful, and I carry myself with class and pride. I'm a dam good mother. I may not have been the best wife, but I was faithful.

On the way home, I didn't even realize tears was falling from my eyes. I didn't even bother to wipe them. My heart was crushed and with each falling tear, I knew in my heart, what I had to do. After I made it home, I sat in the car for a minute and got myself together. I needed time alone to think because even though I was pissed, I didn't want to do anything that would take me away from my children.

I went home and called a moving company. I needed a company that could have the entire house packed up in four hours. I was willing to pay the extra for rushed moving. After securing a moving company and a storage unit to store my furniture, I packed up the kids clothes, shoes, and toys and put them in my car. I called into work and took the day off. Then, I got a room at the Fairfield Marriott hotel. The movers came and move everything to my storage units. After a few hours, the only thing that was left in the house was kitchenware, his clothes, shoes, tools, and I left a TV with a DVD player. I placed the DVD of him and Diamonique on top of the TV for him to watch it before I left and went to the hotel.

For a few hours, I just laid across the bed staring at the ceiling trying to decide what to do, how this was going to affect the kids, would I ever be able to forgive my sister, and husband. There were so many questions and I didn't have any answers.

I must have fallen asleep because when I woke up, it was ten something. I grabbed my phone and I had over fifty calls and messages from Jonathan. I ignored them all and put him on the block list. I had a few texts from Sasha, so I texted her back and let her know that I was okay and that I didn't do anything crazy. I didn't tell her where I was. I just wanted to be alone. I got up and showered and put on some clothes because laying around the room was only pissing me off.

My cellphone woke me up around four a.m. It was a number I didn't recognize, so I ignored it. When the calls started coming in back to back, I knew it was Jonathan. I added that number to the block list as well. There was nothing else to say between us. I endured his disrespect for years hoping and praying that things would get better, only to find out he was banging my sister.

Although it's not going to be easy, I know I have to move on with my life and let go of some things, starting with my husband and my sister. I know eventually I can forgive them, but right now isn't that time.

I read a quote once that said: "Sometimes choosing to live means letting go." Funny how that quote fits my life. For years, my husband and I have been literally trying to force the pieces of this marriage to back together and like cheap glue holding a broken vase together, eventually the pieces came apart again. The story of my marriage, the broken pieces of our hearts, just couldn't be made whole again, but even, after all that, I still loved my husband. I still wanted my family, but I'm learning that something the very thing we want is the one thing hurting us.

*****

It's been three months since I left Jonathan and as much as I want to hate him, I can't because the truth is I still love him. I'll always love him. As much as I bury my pain, as much as I fight the tears, the memories together I just can't seem to erase. I look at our children and it pains my heart that I'm breaking up their family. I know it's crazy for me to take that blame but that's how I feel. Some days I feel like such a failure because my marriage didn't work. Other days, I feel so confused, so bipolar, so lost, so misunderstood. Half of the time, I don't know what I'm doing or what is going on. Days pass and run together, yet like Ralph Ellison, I am the invisible man. Nobody sees my pain. Nobody knows the hurt I feel. Even though I haven't even filed yet, this divorce feels like the grieving process I went through with my dad all over again. It took me over a year to properly grieve and deal with the pain of losing my dad. It almost destroyed me and now it's happening again. My husband and my dad were the only two permanent men in my life and now I've lost them both. No, my husband is not dead but the thought of this divorce is wearing me down like cancer eating at my insides.

For so long, all we had in this world was each other and the thought of being apart and moving on even though it's for the best is so hard. I don't know what to do anymore. Yet going through this divorce feels like grief already. I'm trying to keep it together. I know there is life after divorce, but the hardest part is getting there. I'm not giving up yet and I know in time, I can learn to be happy again

_____

BROTHERLY LOVE

I was at Starbucks sitting under the pavilion, writing and enjoying my caramel Frappuccino when I heard someone call my name.

"Paige Robinson!"

I looked up and locked eyes with Kelvin, who helped himself to a seat at my table. He was still fine as hell. Light-skinned guys were never my type, but Kelvin was the exception to that rule. He's about 5'11 with honey-colored eyes, athletic build body, and the cutest lips, you ever want to see. They aren't too big or too little, it's like he has the perfect set of lips.

"Kelvin Harris!" I replied as I got up to hug him.

"Long time no see or hear from, Paige! I see you still looking good with your slim thick, chocolatey ass! Why I haven't heard from you in a while? Guess you be too busy with my brother to hit me up now!" Kelvin stated.

"Kelvin. What you mean? Why would you say that? I mean I do have a job and a family. I can't kick it like I use to, I have responsibilities now but you know you still my dawg!" I said with a big smile.

"Yea, ok. I hear ya. Just funny how you make time to see my brother, but you always putting me on the backburner. My brother talk about you every time we together. I get so pissed off thinking that it should me talking about how good you taste and feel. Shit, I be wanting to tell him our little secret so bad, but I just can't hurt him like that because I know how he feels about you, even though you already got a man. I'd be lying if I said I'm over joyed at the idea of you being with him. I know you are not my woman, but I miss the shit out of you and what we had. The fact that he doesn't know that once upon a time, you had me feeling the same way he feels, puts me in an awkward position. I'm not going to tell him because I'm not a hater and it's my little brother, but damn baby I miss the fuck out of you!"

"Don't be like that, Kev! You know how I feel about you, but our friendship meant more to me than anything else and I didn't want to hinder that especially after I met and fell for Shaun. Once I found out he was your brother, I had to make a decision because I didn't want to be stuck between two brothers. What you and I had was cool, but it was just casual sex, a friend with benefits type thing. I actually fell for your brother and it became so much more than sex."

"I guess. It's cool, you still my dawg and if being with my brother makes you happy then I'm happy for you because as much as I hate to admit it, he really does love you. I mean he still kicking it with his baby momma and you still with your baby daddy, but he does care for you and I know you care for him. Anyway, enough of that, I'm having a little get together at my house tonight, you should come. My brother will be there, so you don't have to worry about me messing with you," Kelvin stated with a smirk.

"Shaun mentioned he had plans with his baby momma, so if he wanted me there, he would have invited me. I'm not sure if I would want to be around her knowing I'm fucking her man!" I stated.

"Well, if you change your mind, let me know. It was nice catching up with you. Maybe we will run into each other again," Kelvin said and got up.

I watched him get in line and order his drink and left. For a minute, Kelvin looked like Shaun standing there. Even though they were half-brothers, they looked a lot alike. Sometimes too much alike. People always called them ghetto twins in high school, even though they were a year apart.

Memories of Kelvin and I came flooding back. We have been friends since high school. In high school, we occasionally hooked up, but we never let it interfered with our friendship. To me, it was nothing more than a friend with benefits type of thing. During our senior year, we got a new student named Shaun. Shaun and I instantly clicked and we became friends, but it wasn't until after Shaun and I started hooking up that I realized he was Kelvin's little brother.

Kelvin got his coffee and waved goodbye as he was leaving. He put his hand to his ear, gesturing for me to call him. I waved him off and smiled. I started back working on my article for *Exquisite Literary Magazine* to turn into the deputy editor before the deadline.

***

Since the kids were still at my mom's for the weekend, I convinced my boyfriend, Maurrio to attend Kelvin's party with me. I was not going to attend that party alone and have to watch Shaun with his girlfriend all night. Kelvin and Maurrio were cool with each other, but I wouldn't really consider them friends. Maurrio is a year older than Kelvin and I, but in high school they took a few classes together and were on the basketball team together.

We arrived at the party at Kev's house. I decided on a light yellow sheer shirt with beige tank top underneath and khaki casual shorts with wheat-colored wedges. Maurrio had on a white and sky blue striped polo shirt with khaki shorts and white Jordans.

The party was packed. I scanned the room looking for Shaun. People were playing Spades, some were playing Dominoes, a few were playing basketball, and the women was mostly sitting around sipping on mixed drinks. Shaun was nowhere to be found. The grill was going and the DJ was kicking some sweet ninetiess oldies. The party vibe was definitely good, only thing that was missing was Shaun.

The last time Shaun and I hooked up was almost a month ago and although we text and talk over social media, I hadn't seen him in about three weeks. The women were strangers to me and honestly, I had no intention of getting to know them. Kelvin introduced me to the women, but from the look on their faces, they didn't want to get to know me either, so I went to play Spades with the guys. Maurrio didn't want to play cards, so he and Kelvin went to play dominoes. Despite us not being near each other, Maurrio was sure to sit where he could watch me and see if any guys would try to hit on me.

After about thirty minutes or so, Shaun showed up to the party with his girlfriend. It took everything in me to contain my excitement. Shaun had on a yellow, white, and blue polo shirt with khaki shorts, and white high top forces. The aviator shades he wore made him stand out even more than his curly, manly Mohawk hairstyle. Just watching him made me wet. I swear it wasn't planned for us to dress alike. I stole a few glances while playing cards. As I waited on the dealer to finish dealing my cards, for a brief second, our eyes locked and held their own conversation. My mind tried to wonder about the what-if. *What if we didn't have to hide our relationship? What if he was my man? What if Maurrio and I broke up? What if he and his girlfriend break up?* I snapped back into reality and broke our eye conversation and started gathering my cards.

Maurrio knew nothing about me and Shaun or me and Kelvin, and Shaun knew nothing of me and Kelvin, so I planned to keep it that way, despite my body's yearning for Shaun's touch. After the last hand and my team lost in Spades, I got up. I walked over to Maurrio to make sure he was okay and to see if he wanted something to eat.

"Hey baby, you good? You want me to get you something to eat?" I asked him.

"Nah, babe. I'm wait til I finish this game," he replied.

I bent down closer to Maurrio and whispered in his ear, "I'm going to the bathroom and I'm going to get me something to eat afterwards, so I'll be back." Then I kissed him on his neck. "Kelvin, where's the bathroom?" I asked.

"Down the hall, first door on your right." My mom and so more people are inside, if you can't find it, ask someone inside to show you," Kelvin said while his eyes were trying to have their own conversation.

Of course, I knew where the bathroom was, but Maurrio didn't know that and if I hadn't asked where the bathroom was, it would have looked very suspicious. I walked off, headed to the bathroom as the other guys at that table, Kelvin included started joking him about being pussy whipped. Once I got inside, I spoke to Kelvin's mom and aunts and asked them where the bathroom was because I didn't want to just march to the bathroom as if I lived there. His mom showed me where the bathroom was. I thanked her and went inside. I didn't have to use the bathroom, I just needed a moment to get myself together. Seeing Shaun was sending my hormones racing and the sparks were flying so wide between us that it seemed like everyone at the party could see them. I was starting to think bringing Maurrio along was a big mistake. I quickly texted Maurrio and asked if he was ready to go. While I waited on him to text back, I touched up my makeup a little. Maurrio texted back that he wasn't ready to go and that he was actually about to head to the store with Kelvin to get some more beer. I said ok and got ready to exit the bathroom. Before I could exit the bathroom, Shaun rushed in and locked the door.

I started to say something but he ran to me and kissed me before I could say anything. We were playing a dangerous game and although I really cared for Shaun, I had no intentions of us being caught together. I broke the kiss and tried to leave. Shaun continued to kiss me, "Relax" he whispered in between kisses. "Kelvin, took your husband to the store with him and my girlfriend had to leave to go pick up her sister, so we got time."

"What about the people in the living room?" Pushing him away from me long enough to ask.

"Don't worry, they didn't see me come in, they into that show they watching, now come on you wasting time and you know you want this dick just as much as I want that pussy, now stop playing with daddy and bring that azz here!"

The way he said that shit made my panties moistier than a Duncan Hines cakes and before I knew it my shorts and panties were pulled down to my ankle and I was touching my toes while he was fucking the shit out of me! He turned the fountain on in the sink to draw out the sounds. Even though it was a quickie, that shit was amazing. We quickly got ourselves cleaned up and I exited the bathroom first and went into the kitchen and fixed me a plate and went outside to sit at a picnic table to eat.

I wasn't really hungry, but I told Maurrio I was going to get something to eat and he would have suspected something if I didn't have a plate of food. After about ten minutes, Shaun exited the house with a plate of food as well and sat opposite me at the table. We didn't say a word to each other but, the chemistry between us was felt. My phone vibrated and I checked my messages and it was Maurrio letting me know he was on his way back. As I replied back to Maurrio's text, I noticed Shaun texting on his phone. My phone vibrated again and this time it wasn't Maurrio but Shaun. The text read, *that shit was awesome. Damn, I wish you were mines. I'm tired of being your little secret. I want you all to myself!*

Even though, we were directly across from each other, I couldn't risk speaking aloud to him, so I replied to his text, *Shaun, don't do this, especially not here. We will talk about us later, just please don't do anything stupid. Shit you know how I feel too, but you also know the deal between us, so stick to your end of the bargain and yes, that shit was amazing! Now stop texting me, my boyfriend on his way back!*

Thank God for private messaging apps! We ate in silence and Kelvin and Maurrio finally returned from the store. Maurrio walked over and brought me a Hershey's Almond bar and sat down beside me.

"What's up, Shaun?" He asked.

"Sup, Maurrio. I'm good." Shaun stately coolly.

"You ready to eat, Maurrio?" I asked

"Yeah, I'm bout to get something now."

"I'll fix your plate," I stated thankful for an opportunity to leave from in the midst of the hot seat. The song, *The Love We Had Stays on my Mind* by Dru Hill came on and my mind took me back to freshman year of high school when Shaun and I went to the ball together. We danced to that song and I remembered thinking that night that I was going to marry him, but fate had other plans and shortly after that, I met and fell for Maurrio.

I finished fixing Maurrio's plate and took it to him. Kelvin and some more guys had now joined them at the table, so I gave him his plate and went and sat at the picnic table with the ladies. On the way over the Ladies' table, my phone vibrated again. I thought it was Shaun again, but this time it was Kelvin.

The message read, *you owe me! I want to collect my payment later tonight or else! LOL!*

I quickly replied, *Or else what??? And how do I owe you?*

Instead of sitting at the table with the ladies, I found a seat off to myself, so I could see what the hell Kelvin was talking about.

He replied back, *I got rid of your hunny, so you and my brother could share that little bathroom quickie, so now I want my turn.*

I was pissed, this nigga was literally trying to blackmail me out of some pussy! What the hell! Where the fuck do they do that at? My mind was going a million miles a minute to come up with something so that I didn't give myself away and then it hit me. I smiled and text Kelvin back, *Okay, I'm hit you up later tonight. Be ready!* Just as I finished texting Kelvin, *My Little Secret* by Xscape comes on.

It was so many secrets swirling in the air that the atmosphere just felt heavy. I started singing along to the song, stealing glances at Shaun and Kelvin.

By the time it got to the verse about being in the same room with you and your girlfriend, my panties were moist all over again and I knew then at that moment that I had to go before Shaun and I gave ourselves away. I texted Maurrio and told him I was ready to go. He said his goodbyes and we left. I texted Shaun and told him to get a room at our usual place and meet me there around nine. Since I was going out with my girls later that night, Maurrio wouldn't think nothing of me being out late, since my girls' night out always end late. I texted Kelvin and told him to meet me at 8:30 at the club.

*****

It was a little after eight and Kelvin still hadn't shown up yet. I called him and he finally answered that he was on his way.

"Okay, when you get here, just pull on the side. I'm riding with you," I said and hung up.

Kelvin arrived and parked. I got in the car with him and we left to go to the hotel, where unbeknownst to Kelvin, his brother was waiting for me. Kelvin was so happy to finally get another chance, that he didn't even noticed his brother's car in the parking lot. I knocked on the door, which puzzled Kelvin, because I hadn't told him somebody was already in the room. His brother opened the door and they both looked stunned. I walked past Shaun into the hotel room with the double beds. I put my purse on the table and walked to Shaun and kissed him. Shaun kissed me back, but he looked at me and back at his brother and snapped. He started cursing and kept asking what was going on between me and his brother.

I finally admitted to Shaun that Kelvin and I used to hook up before he came to school with us and that I didn't know they were brothers until it was too late and that's when I broke things off with Kelvin for him. I showed him the text message that Kelvin sent me threatening me. I didn't show him the messages, so he could hurt his brother I just wanted him to know what the situation was about. Seeing that Shaun was about to completely go off on his brother. I pulled him to me to stop him from possibly hitting his brother.

"Really, bruh? You would betray me like that?" Shaun was pissed and venom was flying off every word that he spoke.

"It's not even like that man, but I had her first," Kelvin retorted.

"Yea, but you couldn't keep her and she left you for me and we been together ever since. She loves me and you know that, so why would you try to ruin that? Plus, you know how I feel about her?" Shaun exclaimed.

"Look, I think it's best if you leave, before I do something I regret. I love you man, I do but don't every try to interfere with my personal life again. I don't get in your mess with you and your woman, so stay out of mines. If I want to date a woman that already has a man that's my business, but what you not go do is try to use her and blackmail her because of it. So, please just get the fuck out!" Shaun demanded.

I didn't know what to say. I felt bad for Kelvin, but he had to know what he was doing to his brother was wrong. Kelvin left out the door, slamming it behind him, hopped in his car and drove out.

The tears I had been holding in was finally running down my face. "I'm sorry Shaun, I should have been told you. I just didn't know how and I didn't want you to think I was a hoe or something, but I do love you. I love you more than I ever loved Kelvin or Maurrio," I said as the tears came harder and faster.

"It's okay! I love you just as much as you love me. Now we just got to find out what we going to do about that because I want you all to myself, I no longer want to be your LITTLE SECRET!"

For more information about Patti Doss

www.authoresspattidoss.com or
www.exquisitereadspublications.com

Facebook pages:

www.facebook.com/ExquisiteReadsPublications/

www.facebook.com/authoresspattidoss/

Reading Group:

www.facebook.com/groups/ExquisiteBookineers/

Mailing list

https://madmimi.com/signups/145217/join

Email:

exquisitereadspublications@gmail.com

Other Books by Patti Doss

Somebody Else's Husband Series

Somebody Else's Husband: Tammie's Story

Somebody Else's Husband: Persia's Story

Somebody Else's Husband: Rachel's Story

Somebody Else's Husband: Sharon's Story, The Encore (coming Fall 2016)

Novella

Finding Love at Christmas

Anthologies

A Hood Summer Night's Dream

Women Withstanding All